Weekly Reader Children's Book Club presents

Raggedy Ann & Andy™ in The Tunnel of Lost Toys

by Catharine Bushnell
Illustrated by Vernon McKissack

The Bobbs-Merrill Company, Inc.
Indianapolis / New York

Copyright © 1980 by The Bobbs-Merrill Company, Inc.
All rights reserved, including the right
of reproduction in whole or in part in any form.

ISBN 0-672-52633-6
Library of Congress Catalog Card Number: 79-25675
Manufactured in the United States of America

This book is a presentation of Weekly Reader
Children's Book Club, which offers book clubs
for children from pre-school to young adulthood.

For further information, write to:
Weekly Reader Children's Book Club
1250 Fairwood Avenue
Columbus OH 43216

NE SUNNY SATURDAY, Marcella ran into the playroom. "Wake up, Raggedy Ann! Wake up, Raggedy Andy! We are going to the Amusement Park today!"

Raggedy Ann's painted smile grew even wider.

"Oh boy," said Raggedy Andy, "I can hardly wait! I want to go on the roller coaster two hundred times!"

They went on many rides at the Amusement Park.
Raggedy Ann liked the merry-go-round best of all.
Andy liked the Ferris wheel better. It took them up
very high. But it wasn't high enough for Andy.

Late in the afternoon, Marcella said, "Well, Raggedy Ann and Andy, we have time for only one more ride. What shall it be?"

Raggedy Andy opened his mouth to shout out, "The Hurricane Daredevil Roller Coaster, Marcella. That's what I want."

Ann gave him a quick frown and he stopped. After all, no one must know that dolls can talk. Not even for a ride on the Hurricane Daredevil Roller Coaster.

"The Tunnel of Fun!" Marcella exclaimed. "I think we will do that."

"Phooey," Andy muttered. "Little boats on a river. That's going to be boring. A brave, tough boy like me needs *action!*"

Raggedy Ann smiled to herself. She knew that the Tunnel of Fun would give Andy a big surprise.

They settled themselves in a boat. Just as they entered the tunnel, spooky music began to play. Around the corner an eerie light began to glow. Raggedy Andy mumbled, "I don't think very much of this ride so far. . . . WOW!"

He nearly fell off the seat in surprise. A purple witch came screaming out of the darkness. "Maybe this isn't so tame after all," he said. "But don't you worry, Annie, I'll take care of you and Marcella."

The Raggedies' little boat passed many exciting scenes. Vampires and monsters, pirates and skele-tons popped out from all directions. Even Andy's shoebutton eyes were very wide.

The boat turned another corner. Raggedy Ann cried,
"Oooh, I think I hear a waterfall ahead." Sure
enough, there was a very steep slope of rushing water.

Sitting in a cave at the edge of the waterfall was the biggest, fiercest dragon they had ever seen. He had green scales sparkling with gold glitter. His orange eyes gleamed and he breathed blue flames over the water. "Look, Ann," Andy said. "If we go near him, we'll be burned up!"

"Don't worry, Andy," she laughed. "His flames stop just as each little boat passes him. See, it's very safe." But Raggedy Ann was wrong.

Near the dragon's cave hung two long strings. Raggedy Ann felt one of them brush her face as they passed. Suddenly a tiny hook on the end of the string caught in her dress. Andy was hooked too. Both of them were pulled up and left hanging in the air in front of the dragon. It happened so fast that Marcella did not even notice. She sailed away down the waterfall.

"Poor Marcella," said Ann. "She will be very worried. I wonder who put these strings here?"

"I did," said the dragon. He unhooked them very carefully. "You are my prisoners," he growled.

The dragon carried them into a room with a deep hole in the floor. The sides of the hole were much too steep to climb. Many other toys were in the hole. "You will stay here," he told Ann and Andy. And he put them into the pit.

"Why are you doing this?" cried Raggedy Ann.

"My job is to scare people," said the dragon. "Now your friend will be very scared for you."

"That's not the right kind of scared," said Ann. "That's worried-scared, not fun-surprised-scared. People should be happy when they come here."

The dragon was very puzzled. He said, "I must think about this." And he went away.

In the pit, the other toys ran to greet the Raggedies. There was a pink octopus, a crying baby doll, a beautiful ballet dancer, a stuffed dog, a painted rocking horse, and a wonderful cowboy doll with spurs and a big hat.

"My name
is Cowboy Mike,"
said the doll. "Who are you?"

"I am Raggedy Ann. This is my brother, Raggedy
Andy," Ann said. "You poor things. I wish I could
think of a way to help us all."

The wishing pebble in her cotton stuffing heard her
wish and gave her an idea. "I know," she cried.
"Andy is a very brave boy. He is also very light. If
he stands on the head of the rocking horse, and we
all jump on the tail, Andy will fly out of the pit!"
"Yes," said Cowboy Mike, "and he can carry my
rope so that we can all climb out."

Raggedy Andy was not very happy about this. But he bravely climbed onto the horse's head. "OK, jump," he said.

All the dolls jumped very hard on the back of the horse. Andy sailed out of the hole.

Andy lowered the rope. The ballerina climbed up
first. The stuffed dog sat on her shoulders. Dancers
are very strong, so she didn't mind at all. Then Raggedy Ann went up the rope. Cowboy Mike followed.

At the top, Raggedy Ann looked down. "Oh dear," she said, "the baby can't climb. What shall we do?"

The pink octopus waved one of his arms as if to say, "Don't worry." Then he tied the end of the rope around the rocking horse. He put his long arms around the baby doll and carried her up the rope. Everyone cheered. But they did it very quietly so the dragon wouldn't hear. Then all the toys pulled on the rope together. The rocking horse came up too.

They all ran to the door. But when they opened it, the dragon was waiting. He roared loudly and made terrible faces at them. "You cannot leave," he shouted. "I'll eat you!"

Raggedy Ann said, "You can't fool us, Mr. Dragon. We think you are just lonely. That's why you're so mean."

The dragon stopped jumping up and down. "You are right, Raggedy Ann. I have been mean. But how could anyone like a scary dragon?"

"That is very silly," she said, "everyone likes you. Besides, you cannot steal friends."

Just then one of the little boats floated past them.
"Mother, there is the big dragon," a boy said.
"I like him best."

"You see? Everyone who comes on the Tunnel of
Fun ride is your friend," Raggedy Ann said.

"Oh, thank you, Raggedy Ann," said the dragon, "I
must get back to work. I promise I'll remember to be
only happy-surprising-scary from now on."

"Oh, Raggedy Ann, you saved us!" cried the balle-rina. All the toys thanked her very much.

Then Andy said, "How are our owners going to find us? They're not going to look for us in this cave."

"Don't be so gloomy, Andy," said Cowboy Mike. "Your sister Ann is a very good thinker. She will help us."

Raggedy Ann sat down on a rock. Suddenly she jumped up and cried, "I have it! Here is what we do. We must wait until all the people have gone. Then we will run to the Lost and Found Department and sit down on the shelf. I will write a small note to the Lost and Found Man."

Raggedy Ann wrote:

Dear Mr. Lost and Found Man,
    I found these toys in the Tunnel of Fun.
Please take good care of them.
                Handyman Fred

The next morning, the Lost and Found Man was
very surprised indeed. There were eight new toys on
his shelf. He read the note and nodded his head.

"Well, well," he said. "I must put a notice in the
newspaper for the owners of these toys. And these
must be the two Raggedies that Marcella was so
worried about yesterday. I will call her right now."

Back home in the playroom at last, Marcella tucked
Raggedy Ann and Andy into bed. "You two had an
adventure," she said. "You must be very tired. Sleep
well." She turned out the light and closed the door
very softly.

Raggedy Ann sighed sleepily, "How lucky we were to be able to help those toys get back home. We made the dragon happy, too."

But you and I know that the toys were just as lucky.
They made two friends as special as Raggedy Ann
and Raggedy Andy.